Marc Roberts

Listen

First published in Great Britain in 2010 by:
Opening Chapter, 171 Kings Road, Cardiff, CF11 9DE

www.openingchapter.com

All rights reserved

© Marc Roberts 2010
http://myspace.com/zeukx

The right of Marc Roberts to be identified
as the author of this work has been asserted
in accordance with the Copyright,
Designs and Patents Act 1988

A catalogue record for this book is available
from the British Library

ISBN 13: 978-1-904958-14-7

All rights reserved. No part of this publication
may be reproduced, transmitted, or stored
in a retrieval system, in any form or by any
means, without permission in writing
from Opening Chapter.

Cover photo by Noel Dacey
illustrations by Ellie Young
design by WMD walesmediadesign.com

To Freyja

Acknowledgements

In regard to the manifestation of this work, for the encouragement and inspiration I offer my heartfelt thanks to Derec Jones for all his effort, the opportunity, and for daring to *dream*, my Mother and Father, Amanda Roberts, Noel Dacey for condoning it, Don Tatem, the quiet star, The roses Rose and Rosie, Opening Chapter, David Shepherd, Jimmy and Emily, Barry of the Wood, Rhian Jones, Ellie Young, Pamela Wyn Shannon, Alex and Tanja, The Jasmine Fetish, The spirit Zeuk, Fruits de Mer records, Michael Lordofchaos, Hartley, The Shining Ones, Paul Wale, Chapter Arts Centre, Pulse Wholefoods, Y Cardiff, Lynda, L'indolente, and to all the artists and friends I have been moved by and *heard* over the years of discovery.

Marc Roberts May 31st 2010

Foreword

Music and words. Words as music. I have always loved both.

I have been blessed to have been moved to understanding something of the world through them. I have been enchanted to be utterly dislocated from the world by them…

Here are my words…some songs, some poems, some prose.

'The Whispering Wheel' section is a poetic exploration of 'The Tarot', or 'The Devil's Picture book'. The 22 Haiku relate to the 22 trumps of the major arcana, whilst the titles for the other poems are suggested by Crowley's 'Book of Thoth' and relate to certain 'minor arcana' cards.

My musical projects are ever evolving. Something of them can be heard
at www.myspace.com/zeukx
and www.myspace.com/herbrobert

With Love

Marc Roberts

Contents

Listen

Stuff
Herby 2
Herby 3
Two More Poems
The Whispering Wheel
    Haiku
     Other
Lyrics

Listen

STUFF

No Room

four wan
        walls,
a window,
    and a door, stare,

            in silence

   upon
 one naked bed,
one barren shelf,   and
                 one self.

Pie in the sky

Barry Pye, a healthy, handsome, energetic young man, worked in the meat factory. That's what everybody called it, the meat factory. The people of Bumpton regarded it as a fine establishment, producing the tastiest pasties, pies, rissoles, sausages, scratching and speciality burgers anyone could ever hope to savour. In fact, the Bumpton pie had lately become renowned far beyond the small town itself. This led to murmurs among the crew, as the workers called themselves, that expansion and maybe pay rises were imminent.

Barry, a packer, secretly looked forward to, and hoped for, a promotion. He had many plans and dreams. Particularly he looked forward to the day when he would see the ghost of the playful moniker 'Barry Bike' exorcised, and drive to work and back home in a neat car. Black or red it would be, with a nice interior and a wicked stereo. But as it was, and as it had been for some time, he'd arrive at and leave the factory that day on the Eagle. A sturdy two wheeled wonder his father had fondly handed down saying 'she served me well for years son, and there's life in the old horse yet.'

It was a sunny Friday. Barry had been on days, and clocking off at 3.30, had decided to go to The Crown with some of the crew for a pint. One pint became two and three. 3.30 became 5. Then Barry thought it was time to go home for tea. Fish and chips and peas it would be. Finishing his lager and saying 'see you later' to his mates, Barry left the pub, unlocked the Eagle, and pedalled onto the road home in a comfortable haze.

But Barry didn't see his friends later, or make it home for tea.

He'd got to the crossroad at Western Way and rightly stopped at a red light. He considered whether he'd get across the road quicker if he used the pedestrian crossing as he sometimes did. Then as if his mind had given him space to think, he thought about Julie, and whether he would see her again, and if he did, would she speak to him even.

Julie was Barry's true love. They'd first met one Saturday night in a loud and crowded Stardust club. She was a nurse and had been out with a friend, Sandra. Sandra had copped on with Jon, Barry's mate, and Barry was left feeling quite awkward with Julie at a table loaded with empty and half empty glasses. The pair of them watched Jon and Sandra kiss and grope each other on the dance floor, and chatted about pies and hospitals.

The following week the same happened. Barry and Julie found they had much in common, and became fond of each other.

Barry mused on those early meetings with an almost aching melancholy as he stared at the red light above and before him.

The odds were astronomical. Most people were baffled. Many were alarmed. But nearly all were sorry for poor Barry. Such a nice young man. Such a promising future. Such a cruel fate.

The police had called to 32 Pleasant view at 6.30. Mrs Pye, suspicious at first, let them into the narrow hallway, and closed the door on a mellow evening. She listened with a creeping dread as a policeman reported in concerned yet firm tones that there had been an accident. He assured Mrs, and having heard the commotion in the hallway, a cramped and cardiganed Mr Pye, that everything was all right. Everything that could be, was being done, and doctors expected Barry to regain consciousness soon.

However, when it came to explaining what had happened, even the officer, familiar with such delicate situations, had difficulty in keeping a professional and rational tone to his voice.

No witness was able to give a clue as to what had occurred. The driver of the Escort beside Barry said he thought the cyclist looked a little unsteady perhaps. That one second he was there, then he was not. It was a passenger in the car behind the Escort who saw him go down, and called the emergency services. By examining the wound, they could only come to the conclusion that something had fallen from the sky, and hit Barry on the head, out of the blue. There were no buildings that near to the road for anyone to have thrown something from, and why on earth would anyone have done that? Yet no appropriate object could be found, despite the enthusiastic searching by officials, motorists and some interested passers by.

The logical and accepted explanation was that a lump of ice had done it. 'Blue ice' probably from an aeroplane. It must have shattered upon impact, then melted and dried up before anyone realised what had happened.

Luckily, the expensive visits to the hospital were fairly short lived. So too was any patience and understanding on the part of Barry's friends and family.

The golden leaves in the park near Barry's home were becoming a crispy carpet for kicking kids. They would reluctantly run home through them to soak up some soap operas, game shows or situation comedy classics, and munch on a Bumpton burger or pie perhaps. Barry would sit on a bench in the park and stare at the long shadow of his favourite tree until a creeping park keeper told him the park was closing and he had have to leave.

Some people said Barry no longer followed the plot, or got the joke. That he had lost it. Not that the doctors could find anything wrong with him. Of course, the knock had done it, but he had, well, changed. Those that didn't laugh at him, or ignore him, treated him like a helpless child. Barry's response to any of these approaches was the same, a hazy indifference.

Maybe it was the waxing winter, or the increasingly frequent downpours which kept Barry away from his slatted graffitied throne in the park. Perhaps any cobwebs which had clung to Barry's mind after the accident were blown away along with the leaves which were heaped up in sad piles against the rusted railings., like leftovers of a plentiful feast, or the litter of a carnival show. Whatever, with the change in the weather came an even greater change in Barry's manner.

He redecorated, or rather undecorated his room. This caused some alarm for his mother who thought such sudden and drastic action unhealthy. His father took an opposing view of it. He tried to comfort Mrs Pye, and told her to leave him to it. He was too old now to have pictures of footballing heroes, sports cars and sexy film stars clinging to every inch of wall and ceiling.

But soon Barry's morose behaviour and dark aura began to touch both the Pyes. Sensing it's contagious potential, Barry was left to his own devices, and if any, only the most essential attention was paid to him.

Barry had taken to wearing black, and only black every day. His hair had grown over his ears and his fingernails were noticeably longer than they ever had been. What had been frequent lapses into reverie was now a permanent state of being.

Mr and Mrs Pye really didn't know what to do, so coming to a decision that he'd snap out of it in time, they got on with things as they had done, and life went on.

You would hardly have noticed that Barry was there, and if you had seen him staring at himself in the hallway mirror, mouthing words to his wan reflection with the intensity of a certain accusation, you would have made believe to yourself that he wasn't really there.

One afternoon Mrs Pye heard running water, the squeak of taps turned tight and a solitary splash come from the bathroom. She washed her hands, wiped them on her pinny and took up the rare opportunity to have a look inside Barry's room. It was a taboo which had not been broken. Partly due to the advice of doctors, partly due to the strange silence. With polish and duster in hand, she walked into the room, switched on the light and was quite amazed. There in the corner stood a wooden frame. Attached to that frame was a canvas. Upon that canvas was an image, and that image was simply hideous.

When Mrs Pye regained her composure, and straightened her mind and pinny, the surprise before her became plainly what it was. A painting. That almost explained it. At least it made some sense. She wasn't exactly sure why, but suddenly the sullen moods, the solitude, the silence was somehow justified. Barry had taken up art. Yes it was strange. It was unbelievable. It was almost impressive. She'd seen this kind of thing on a TV program. Not all artists painted pretty flowers and cottages.

She heard a glug, glug and schlurrp sound across the landing, came to her ordinary senses, and discreetly left the room.

Later that evening she told Mr Pye about her discovery. From behind the black and white wall of the Bumpton Herald, he told her at least Barry was doing something with himself. Then muttered something about there being an E. Coli crisis at the meat factory. He was by now neither curious or concerned about Barry. Barry's own curiosity and concern was another matter. It was with his paintings.

He created six paintings, and only the most discriminating eye could have noted any variation between them. That is if each had not been destroyed. Each completed canvas, each pastel perfection splattered with a thick black oily gunk. Slashed, sliced, slaughtered with a cruel Stanley knife. The debris set alight and burnt to cinders in a metal bin in the yard after dark.

Completing each piece, which was decided upon by a feeling as alien to Barry as painting, he would allow the work to rest there on it's tripod for a few days, and allow himself to tumble through the vortex of colours. He would gaze into it night and day, tormented by a feeling that there was something he just had to remember. The moments, minutes, hours, days and nights of frustration had more than once resulted in Barry letting out a wail which terrified his parents, and neighbours. In the heavy silence which ensued, Barry would attend to the ritual of destruction. This hurt as much as it satisfied him The decomposure ending with fine ashes flitting about his head and falling onto barren flower beds.

One Sunday afternoon there was a knock on the door. Mr and Mrs Pye were out for the day, visiting relatives. Barry ignored the first knock. He thought it would be those strange people who sometimes called around on a Sunday being ever so friendly. They would tell him all about the apocalypse , and how if he brought some books, and went for coffee, he would be saved. Sometimes they frightened Barry. When Barry started to frighten them, they stopped calling. They still sometimes posted those magazines with pictures of smiling children and cute animals in sunny valleys though.

He heard the third knock and dropped the purple pastel he held. A strange feeling rose slowly from his stomach to his chest, from his chest to his throat, from his throat to his head. Then almost in a frenzy he left the room, ran down the stairs and opened the front door. The first thing he felt was the cold. The first thing he saw was the snow. It floated down. A soft, white, silence. It sparkled on the hedge, the gate and in the hair of the woman who stood there. Her lips were frozen in a half smile which was then broken by a wispy mist and the word 'Barry'. At once he felt a chill keener than any blizzard and sharper than any hail storm. The voice did it. Seeing her aroused a feeling with which Barry had become very familiar. But when he heard that single simple word which meant everything and nothing, which he somehow knew, yet didn't...he was overcome.

Powdered Words (nothing emerges)

in the twilight before the elder night forgotten remembered eggs crack dogs bark and faces are smeared bloody children drip black horror and terrify the rich and poor whose mantra is zombic my heart thumps thunderous the walls are ice my hands are burning there are cats and turtles universal are you sleeping is your horror let us sing of horror from bony plinths on crowded high streets you do not need glasses to hear the finely tuned ugliness nor a trumpet to see the discord of beauty my eyes see the day and the fakers who would do well to collect feathers we rest our elbows on dead moons sometimes we whisper or shout with opaque eyes so much time is taken up learning and nurturing guises the glass cracks now my hands are damp everybody looks afraid the circus it seems is a lot more fun than real life the lions are hungry the meat is rotting.

the glad flower could easily be crushed by mechanical impulses heavy words are thrown like wishing stones into foetid fountains we create ourselves without heart and are cruel we move without thought our nerves are taut or slack fortunate or unfortunate it depends if i tell myself where i am it will ruin an illusion am i locked out i can prove who i am by a picture with a hook kiss my mouth see the mask rip my feet are dusty here there are a severe lack of aliens many fanatics stare at the sky with tired eyes we suck air make beautiful noises glaciers melt and slide rocks are powdered the drake drags its tail across the skymould grows on portraits hung in futuristic galleries new dances are invented but the olden ones are the golden ones one day i will play a hard man for a laugh here there are angels it is all greedy blue look up they are flapping their wings tongues are weaving intricate webs silky and purple in their sacred mouths there is so much talent in the world each sketch is unique i will return as a singer to an audience thirsty for wormwood through a sickly mist i see the story change the light dissolve and suddenly i am old with a passion for flight and the weird i go like this with my head i go like this i go

Teacher

They hit me
Inside,
With words
Hard as the assembly hall floor.

They cut me
Out,
With silence
Sharp as Mrs Thomas' devotional screeching.

Weekday mornings
Bound me,
Aching and bored
At the end of a uniform
Line of boys
Who would be men.

We sat in rows,
At desks inscribed
With legends like –
'Mandy Jones is a fat slag' and,
'Barry Smith sucks cock'.
I once etched a winged heart
Pierced by a flaming arrow,
Which soon became obscured
By the name of some popular
Death metal band.

Before us,
You'd stand
Dishevelled and tired,
In a jacket, cords and cravat.
Cool.
I thought.

One day you acquired a new name...
'Hand Job'
For something
You were allegedly
Caught doing in a stationary cupboard,
At lunchtime.

I kept the Velvet Underground and Zappa tapes
You recorded for me

You packed it in.
And I Looked forward
To the day i would walk
Through those gates
For the last time,
And scatter so many
Torn and useless words
Beneath a wide,
Late summer sky.

**The day Christopher Reeves
Had an accident**

Lilly sucks a strawberry ice,
Her lips are cracked
And bleeding.
Her teeth are smashed.

A limping man
Clutching a brittle carrier bag
To his chest with one hand,
Chokes on some super strength,
Spoiling some nice reject
Summer dresses
With a fine, golden spew.

The radio cackles –
A good old classic.

11.27 –
The swinging doorway to the city.
Plenty of cars and busses,
But no breeze.

One minute to midday.
No bells,
Just sirens,
A fallen superman,
And a plague of hangings.

The Hapless Bat

In your dreamscape
Crowned creature
Of the mysterious,
More treachery and tears
Than laughter and love
By being neither
There nor here

Small, dark, quick, sharp,
I, the hunter
Rising at dusk
See the day die with glory.

I hear your silhouette,
I dart at your head,
And here, trapped,
In your geometry
With circular uncertainty,
I scream

HERBY#2

Angel

The room was small. A black drape, embroidered with a silver emblem hung over the door. It covered the peeling white crosses that fenced in the frosted glass. On the window sill, against the backdrop of the black curtains, a company of crystals, stones and glass objects surrounded a clay vase holding a brittle red paper flower. Opposite the curtains, a weathered mass of wood leaned against the side of the wardrobe. A dismantled television, set upon a table, lay beside a lamp. Above this, a painting of a woman hung.

Michael got undressed and switched off the lamp. He held the painting in his mind's eye until by the time he pulled the red blanket up to his chin, the image had gone. It did feel strange, but that was how he knew the work was complete.

In the morning, he heard Jane and Linda chatting and the front door close. Then he got out of bed.

He finished his coffee, put on his boots and zipped up his black leather jacket.

There was a cue in the post office. Then he picked up his prescription, and sat in the chemist. An elderly woman wearing a navy mac, brown trousers and sandals hobbled in. She sat down and between coughing fits, mumbled to herself about this and that. Then she turned to Michael. "What do you want here fucker?" Michael examined the display of perfume and pills and saw, through a multicoloured lollipop tree, the pharmacist busying himself.

"Thank you". The pharmacist handed the package to Michael.

Back at the house, Michael tried to read, but couldn't. Instead, he lay down, his eyes fixed on the painting. He closed his eyes and thought he could perhaps improve it.

The next day, he walked into town.

"That was a sigh and a half." Michael was startled by the woman's words. His eyelids fluttered behind round, blue tinted shades. He picked up the bag and coins on the counter and walked out of the shop.

Michael put away the paints and poured himself a cold beer. It was unusual for Michael to drink beer in the afternoon, but it was a special day.

He thought about Jane sharing the same birthday. Apart from that and the kitchen and bath, they had nothing in common and had never got on.

The phone rang again as he carefully emptied another bottle into his silver tankard. He heard the tape in the answering machine wind and click, followed by the familiar bleep, bleep, bleep...

A violet candle was alight on the table and the painting rested on a wooden easel. Michael looked at himself in the mirror. He saw a smudge of crimson paint on his cheek, drew his hand across his face, and sat on the bed.

Some time passed. Michael heard music coming from the sitting room and people chatting on the landing. He opened a bottle of brandy and took a swig.. Then he picked up a brush of the table.

When the door opened he turned, and saw a woman staring at him.

"Hi."

His heart thumped.

"What are you painting?"

Michael felt his mouth tighten.

The woman stepped into the room and looked at the painting.

"Who is it?"

Michael shifted and stared into the candle flame.

"She's beautiful. Would you like a smoke"?

Michael sat on the bed, let the smoke slide out of his mouth, and felt his hands tingle.

"I'm Tara." She moved from the painting, pulled back a curtain, and looked out of the window.

"Have you seen the moon tonight?"

Michael picked up the brandy and offered it to Tara.

"No thanks." She selected a green stone from the display and held it in her palm towards Michael. Then she closed her fingers and shut her eyes.

Michael watched her breath fall and rise, and saw her eyes moving behind translucent lids. He closed his eyes, leaned back and felt a breeze on his face.

When he opened his eyes, Tara was looking out of the window, had taken her coat off and was naked. She had found the cards behind the curtain and was shuffling them slowly.

"When is your birthday?"

Tara was looking at a card.

"I know you are Cancerian."

She returned it to the pack.

"I know it is today."

Tara turned, sat on the bed, and threw the cards over her shoulder. She looked at Michael, held his hand and traced the lines on it with her thumb.

Tara kissed Michaels' hand.

Michael looked at Tara, and smiled.

The End

Eat my words

Ghost kitten
You shine easily
Understanding confusion
And emptiness
And the astral door

Why don't you leave me
Or believe me
Blood flow beat
And the curtain closes
Upon an empty stage

Bound by thunder
I have kissed you
You have crowned me
As rain fell upon us

We overtook silence
With hollow words
Distorted
Whispered deeply

Your teeth sharp and keen
How long ago was now
As we went searching for a moment

Wild eyed and wondering
Wired and bewildered
Because we chew
Each precious poisonous word
Until we have nothing to say

Faces as Flowers (Roberts / Tyack)

Faces as flowers getting younger
For the great calling love in real force
To be heard in the garden dreaming of singing
Sung at the dawn spring willing and yours
And at the leaf turn you each turn
Amber horizon journey for more
Infinite sunkiss doubtful dulls
Through winters frostbite pleasure restored
Flowers as faces holding each mind
Blossom of tide turn curving yellows
Ocean of deep love bagging we call
Look to the skies...
Look to the skies...
Look to the skies...we fellows
And my love inside
Quickly to rise
Flowers as faces
Turn your eyes to the sky

Now

Still

She is wondering
That river is silence
    and a shadow is creeping in

Suddenly

He left town
The house is empty
    and full of secrets

Now that I am blind

Now that I am blind
My hand, groping,
For yours,
Feeling not sure
Of any feeling,
Sometimes feeling too sure.
You knowing
I cannot see...
Deep down this is me.
Me knowing
You feel as sure
As I am afraid
Of the dark.

Shamarash

Many slender green arrows rooted on a slope , point seriously skywards. As one they are silent and still. Or as one they whisper and sway.

I, Shamarash, have my dwelling at the foot of this vertical maze. In a shade behind a shimmering silver veil, I sing, I dance.

My song is my name – Shamarash, Shamarsh, Shamarash. I am my dance.

Thirsty ferns come close with chamomiles and bony foxglove. Fresh vibrant grasses surround me. Velvety mosses cling to the wall of my chamber.

Before me, through this curtain of flowing light, the so grand greys rise graceful and majestic. It is when the great golden one climbs onto the back of the crab, that their song rings brightest.

Below the grey ones, the living veil crashes into itself, to go to a place where my sisters, the Sirens, sing songs more mysterious than mine.

I am beauty. You cannot sing over me, but with me. You cannot see my dance and hate me. Yet you come fast to my palace in your dirty metal boxes, leave me ugly offerings after taking freely of my essence. Sometimes you bring huge black bulging bellies to me, which give rebirth to the dead and forgotten. Metal and meat rust and rot. Porn and plastic choke and clog.

Still, I sing on...as do my sisters, the Sirens.

Observation

Looking up...

The slug slow
Grey green sky slides sideways

It bursts

A sliver of blue
Burns for a while
Like the root
Of a dying candle flame
In an empty room

Now that weak
Uncertain shine
Has certainly faded
There is no thing
That is not
Changing

Looking out...

Old folk hunched up tight
On high steps of houses
Concern creases their faces
Bomber Jones is dead
They carted him off this morning
He went in his sleep
They said
Peacefully
Some time last week

Outside…

So the night swallows

The last morsel
Of day
And spits out pips of fire
That are scattered in patterns
Across an alien lazuli terrain

Or so it seems to me

Here

High above the phosphorous glow of towns

Here

Between green and deeper green

A shadow shape
Weird by weird shadows
That whisper
And shake

Shelter

The night horse crept back to sleep

There you are
You are there
Black and white
Straight and strange

I bite my tongue

I cry
You laugh
As the sun set with serious intent

In the end

Soul alone

Snow is smothering the homes of those I'll never know
My mind muffled with a longing
It is cold
Angels shiver
Frost upon their tongues

Silent night

Think about knowing someone as much as I know
Escape the city
The longing for hope

It is hot as hell here
Do your dance with flaming tongue
Burn down the city

There's longing in my soul

The calm relic

Dusk smouldering
Or the light being wild
In the damp evening
Valley dogs bark
Intoxicated trees are
Drowsy with the unthinkable

Jig a moon sadness
Spinning top madness
Myself to myself again
Clutching for clues
Whilst heading home to cloud land

I can't explain myself
Nor any of this
Punch drunk at midfright
Through tear stained windows
Twitching stars are falling

Wanderers at sea

pause at the peak of my climb
   And dive in spiral shift
     Towards
     The great sea

My wings cut thin air and time
   And glide in silent grace
     With ease of energy

I turn against the wind to rise
   And soar
     Towards
      The
      Star
      Of
     Majesty

What's going on

Hallucinations
Seeing the real
Scolded for picking up a cat
Running around on the lords' day

Hallelujah!

The eternal fire escape
Mary in ashes
Blue blood in my top hat
What's going on

HERBY#3

Beauty

Adam had not seen Rose for at least a year. She had kept in touch. The occasional phone call, letter and dream...

It came from everywhere. Her voice pulsated. It smothered his own shriek. He fell, a silent scream in a sea of echo...

Though he missed her, and their excursions together, he considered it over. In many ways they were the perfect partners. Each willing to explore and expand each other's thresholds and limits. Until he cracked.

He was still unable to recall what it was that caused the blackout. What it was that caused him to chase Rose out onto the street at dawn. Screaming and naked. There was no more polite "Hello, how are you?" from the neighbours, and the incident was never mentioned in any of Rose's vague communications. Now, in a post script to one of the weird poems she sometimes sent, she had asked if he'd like to meet up. Fear and longing fused in the pit of Adam's stomach. It created an electricity which had him buzzing around the room clutching the request. Like a lost man looking for something misplaced, having forgotten what it was.

They arranged to meet in the Electric Café, a neutral space on the high street. Rose was sat opposite a pinball machine. The slogan 'Space Destroyer' flashed in red and blue over an image of an F type jet fighter. Two boys slapped and thumped the machine. They brushed past Adam, shouted "Freaks" and ran out. He ordered a coffee and sat down. A girl in a blue check overall went over and put a steaming cup on the table in front of him. He watched her walk away.

"I thought you might have forgotten." Adam looked at her. Her eyes were as deep and as dark as ever they were. Her voice as rich and enchanting. She moved forward. Her hands held his. They felt cold against the heat of the coffee.

"I'm glad I didn't."

"I'm glad you didn't."

He felt pressure against his hands. He wondered if he meant what he said.

Rose lit a cigarette, and took a deep drag. "I've got something special. I think you'll like it. It's different." She blew smoke through puckered pencilled lips. Then she reached into a bag on the chair beside her, and put a box on the table. The box was rose wood, decorated with golden flowers and punctured jade patterns. That wave swept over him again. He knew they wouldn't just meet and talk about music, friends or the weather.

"What is it?" He felt he had been through this before. He recalled the mushrooms, the mantras, the toad juice, the tantra. The irresistible temptation. The arousal of some ancient instinct. She stubbed the cigarette out, leaned towards him, and whispered, "I call her, Beauty." She kissed his ear and withdrew into the chair.

Adam unclasped the box and saw inside it, a spider. It's limbs reached the edges of the purple silk on which it rested, motionless. It appeared to have twice the number of legs expected of such a creature. After a while, Adam realised there were two of them in there. "The one underneath is its skin. It sheds it every other day. That's the part you eat." Rose was leaning over the box. Her hair a curtain of secrecy surrounding it. Black as its contents. Adam stood up, walked to the counter and asked if he could use the toilet. He turned the tap and let the cold water splash off his hands into little puddles on the floor. He turned to the hand drier and switched it on. The air rushing out was almost too hot and deafening. He saw his face distorted in the shiny metal machine. It stretched his features to near implosion. His forehead must have come to a point over the upper curve. His eyes almost reaching the outer edges of the thing. His mouth looked like the bulb of a flower. It opened and the word came out, "Beauty!"

Rose was smoking a cigarette when Adam sat down again.

"My brother Lucky…"

" That mad bastard."

"He brought it back from his travels. He's been off tracing his roots. Try it." She stood up and put on her coat. "You'll like it."

He picked up the box, paid for the coffee and walked out of the café.

Beauty was back in the box on the bedside table. It was more the handling than the eating of the shell that caused Adam's flesh to creep. It didn't taste rancid, like the toad juice. In fact, it was much like eating the dried banana chips he virtually lived on.

He lay down on the bed, switched off the lamp, and closed his eyes. Then his head began to vibrate, with strange sound emanations. Then he could see…

A blue sky flecked with silver and gold lights. A green desert. Then the rain fell. The droplets of rainbow light splashed onto the sand. Each droplet became an elegant shoot. Each shoot a beautiful singing flower. Until he was overcome by a multitudinous moving chorus of colour…

He had been able to think of nothing else. The incredible feeling had stayed with him. The following evening, Rose called around.

"…and i've felt just amazing since."

Rose smiled.

"I told you you'd like it." She poured another glass of wine.

"We can go together."

"How?"

 "Beauty"

Adam handed Rose the box. She took out the carcass, snapped it in two, and gave half to Adam. They broke the legs from the body, and one at a time, popped them into each other's mouth. Then the main body, and finally the head. They finished what was left of the wine.

They sat opposite each other. A low, gentle hum contained in the inches between their faces. Their hands held lightly together, bridging the space between their entwined legs. Light flickered in their eyes. There was a shiver between them. Then they began to sing. Low and slow at first. Then rising in pitch. Gaining momentum. Expanding to fill the whole atmosphere. The gulf between their bodies lessening with each moment, until they collided, and were there...

From their fingers, now petals of some celestial bloom, a stream of silver and gold light rippled as it flowed. It spiralled above them, merged in a single glittering ovoid that cracked, and showered them with a ringing brilliance.

A spidery song in the web of some distant place...

Over

She called over tonight
to collect the clay heads,
dressing gown, hair brush
and bottle of perfume.

She left the hairbrush
and the perfume on the kitchen table,
beside a tear soaked tissue,
and the Peter Hammill records she returned.

Proverb

Birds of a feather
Laugh at so many broth cooks
Dead grass is greener

The Bird

A car alarm stole Robert from his dream. In the dream he had run through a field. A lush meadow home to many flowers. Here he saw sunflowers, there he saw moonflowers. Others, less abundant and more delicate than those sun and moonflowers, drew Robert's attention with their amethystine radiance. When Robert knelt to be closer to one of these, he heard a sound. He looked upwards to see what this airy applause could be, and, where it had been clear and blue, that is everywhere, the sky was now white as chalk. Bone white and beating with the wings of so many birds.

Robert got out of bed, opened the curtains and peeped through an egg shaped tear in the nets. Across the square, old Mrs Jones was struggling to free Harry. Harry had managed to get one of his little bobbly legs stuck in between the spokes of a wheel of her shopping trolley. Robert knew Mrs Jones lived alone. He had never seen her talk to anybody, apart from Harry, at least in the square. And, he had only once seen her without her trolley.

That had been one Sunday afternoon.

Robert had spent the morning making a paper plane. Decorated with swirls and stars, he thought it almost too good to fly. The square was quiet. Robert guessed that the people who lived in the flats which bridged numbers 23 and 13 were out. The balcony made for a great launching pad. He climbed up the stairs, over the black bags spewing litter at the top of them, and from the centre of the ledge, let fly his colourful creation. It soared and swooped and spun and looped. Then, caught by a phantom breeze, disappeared from Robert's sight. Robert was certain it had flown into Mrs Jones's garden. He knew what he had to do, and though terrified, he soon found himself dropping from the scratchy red brick wall into the unknown.

The plane was there. It had landed at the far end of a strip of concrete which ran from the back door to the wall.

Almost feeling safe in the knowledge that he could not possibly be seen through the misty glass of the door ahead of him, Robert inched his way forward his hands either side of the taught shadow of the washing line. Robert stopped, looked up and saw a plastic bag hanging on the line. He stood up, stretched up on his tip toes, jumped, and pulled the bag free of the line. The bag fell heavily onto the concrete. The bag burst at his feet. A jumble of meat and bones spilled out. That very instant, the back door was opened by a curious Mrs Jones who stepped into the garden, and onto the paper plane. A yapping Harry soon followed, and catching a whiff of the delightful mess, made straight for it. By this time Robert was licking his chafed hands, while his father got up from in front of the television to find out who the hell was hammering on the front door on a Sunday afternoon.

That happened at the beginning of the summer holidays. No sun, nor moon rose or set without Robert thinking about that day, Mrs Jones, and her bag of meat. He had much time to think too, since the accident. That happened on the way to the shops. He was to go straight there, buy a packet of cigarettes (he had been given a note) and a paper and come directly back. But he didn't come straight back, because instead of using the underpass, Robert tried to cross the road. It wasn't that bad. He woke up in a hospital bed, with one leg in plaster and cuts on his arms and face. The driver of the car sent a card with £5 in it, the cuts soon healed, and the crutches had become almost fun.

Yesterday they were finally returned to the clinic. To celebrate his father asked if he'd like to go to town for a burger and chips treat. Robert said yes, but could they walk, and go through the little wood on the way. Or maybe go to the pond. Robert liked to sit at the water's edge, and watch the ducks and swans.

The tarmac trail was shiny and sticky. Off the trail, in the wood, Robert felt like he was in a dream. He studied the shapes made by the many branches of the trees, and the blue sky between them. He watched birds rest on those branches, and fly through those spaces. He saw his father stand still and shift the earth with his foot. Then he saw a tiny bird, hop hoping away from the invading boot. Robert ran towards the grounded creature. It stood there, blinking and frozen in the dappled light. Then in an instant, the rock hit it. To Robert the wood felt cold, was silent and dark. His father lifted the rock to review the well aimed action. There they stood for a long time, beneath the branches, and the spaces between the branches.

Two More Poems

A Kiss

Once upon a crescent shining
Over tall chimney pots
We wandered with cats and dogs
Through the lawless night

The Rose was red

'This is not me' you said
Where is your body?
The sea is far away
But I remember the tip toe dare
And you held my face
To kiss me

The Day Pass

Composing beauty
Symbols of sickness and joy
Disgusted, delirious
I sense it
But cannot pass the moon
Or time
And we are the tide

Peace and purity
In the shadow self
Where soft rain sings
We are glassy eyed
And hide ourselves from ourselves

Words flutter
Now all views are remote
Wake up! Listen!
This is your voice

Clutching at doors
Whilst popping to the perpendicular
With thunder in our hearts
And confetti consciousness

All part of the kaleidoscope
My first thought was imaginary
Whilst back on earth
We are all at sea
Open and inimitable

The bright night is yours
Glad dragon

Listen

The Whispering Wheel

Inspired by 'The Devil's Picture Book'

HAIKU

The Fool

Bright child pure of air
Blossom wife of morning sky
Bud of mystery

The Magician

Maker of magik
Memory and thought in flight
Mask of hidden eye

The High Priestess

Seer of the still pool
Serene in the shroud of night
Sacred in movement

The Empress

**Abundance of Earth
Art of beauty love of life
All mother of birth**

The Emperor

**Father of fire
Face severe from victory
Force of right action**

The Hierophant

**Tradition of truth
Taught with blessing of wisdom
Turning of the key**

The Lovers

**Angel of the air
Animating the dead heart
Awakening choice**

The Chariot

**Thunder of the path
Throwing lightning at giants
Through sharp hail and snow**

Justice

**Truth and clarity
Tearing veils of illusion
Throne of scales and sword**

The Hermit

**Withdrawn grey wisdom
Wandering silent shadow
Watcher of rainbows**

The Wheel of Fortune

**Three sisters weaving
Time becoming gone
The whispering wheel**

Strength

**Frenzy of the dance
Flaming passion joy of lust
Fruit of ecstasy**

The Hanged Man

Head toward the root
Hung high in the windy ash
Holding strange runes

Death

Decapitator
Doorkeeper of forever
Destroyer of skin

Temperance

Sunshine and raindrops
Synthesis of light and dark
Song of alchemy

The Devil

Adversary shines
Archangel of fallen light
Androgynous fire

The Tower

Shocking the structure
Shower of enlightenment
Swift strike of fire

The Star

Song of Astara
Shining hope of midnight sky
Source of love and light

The Moon

Mother of the dead
Maiden of blood and water
Mistress of strange light

The Sun

Seed of unsleeping
Spirit of the dream vision
Scorching eye of day

Judgement

Rebirth of the soul
Reaching the death of an age
Rising from water

The World

**Daughter of the wave
Divine dance of union
Dawn of the bright child**

Others

Abundance

Naked
We dance
In moonlight glow
Our airy bodies kiss
And the clouded choir whisper
A deep song
Unknown
Enthroned
In starry show
Our eager eyelight burning
And the Queen of Water rising
From a silent lake
We sing
We dance
We celebrate

Completion

Over the green crown
            and the strong ox,
before the warrior strides
            the glistening moor -
moist with the kiss of the spring tide,
                      the dove flies.

Defeat

To fight,
To bleed,
To weep hot tears,
The salty foam of
Fierce seas.

Friends fall,
Shadows stalk the storm,
The pusillanimous pirate
Ensues.

Disappointment

Damp sands
     Grey dawn
    Static
The storm
Holds its bitter yawn
       Washed eyes
    Forlorn
      Root torn
Kissed black
By the fierce scorpion

Dominion

A tiny world
Held in a hot hand
A fist full of fire,
Away from the sea,
Free to create new slave machines.

Futility

Nowhere.....
      Anywhere.....   Somewhere

A calling
    A howling window,
Well torn shoes
    A fire at the foot
Of a mountain.

    Apparition,
A watery sky light,
    Soaking skin,
       A bone white candle
Between grey fingers

Happiness

Brim full of
Light full
Mind full of
Heart
Eye full of
Light full
Sight full
Of love
Night full of
Light full
Wine for the
Glass
Drunk full of
Light full
Depth of
The draught

Luxury

High is the aged
          Moon
    In her house of water
    Within
       And beyond
             Two
          Stone towers
           Loops of why
  All spinning wheels
Stand still
  Intimate
    Stars are dim
      In the canopy
        Of
          Cloud
          Scud
           Sky

Oppression

The bent back
Of man
Clutching at straws
Twists
Then snaps
Before his burden falls

Peace

Curtain down,
    Nothing
      To be seen.
     Fade,
       Flight,
         Dream,
     A lunatic trip tip,
           Silence.

Power

Mystery spirals
Born of an invisible valley
Dance.
Entering sea - bright – space,
The maelstrom is contained.
Elements awaken
The heart – house quakes.
Crystallisation,
Dimensions embrace.

Ruin

Arrows of day
Impale cold flesh
Desolate man
Lies dead
Ignorant
Of the chosen few
Jaws of heaven
Chew

Satiety

A river flows
Below a rainbow
Children dance
A -ring – a – rose
Upon the earth
We stand together
Ever up
To grow

Strife

Who has known worthwhile battle,
Made shapes of war,
Torn flesh,
Broken hearts
And heads,
Crawled naked from the apex,
To be grounded
By a stronger force,
Unarmed against those
With no free hand,
Those intent
Tooth and claw
On destruction.

Dogs chase their tales
Vultures fly in circles
Here is home,
Reality,
Return,
Eternal flow.

Success

A dim luminance
In a mountainous twilight

Beggars glad as gold
Have their day

A ghost rider glides
Across a stream

Exhausted and drunk
A poet dreams

Swiftness

Flaming Iris!
    We vessels of gold
        Hold you
Prismatic rays
      Amaze our sight
On bright days

Archer of light!
     Aim of the starry
        Night sky
Cloak of fog glow moon eye

The Earth Queen

I am flesh and bone
In my green garden the goat leaps
And the virgin sings
By the white thorn.

I am the beating
Of the mystery drum
In all things,

I am heart
In motion
My kiss
Is strength

The Fiery Queen

I am blood
And gorse
Radiant with experience
Transformed
High with knowledge
Of passion
In my field
Star flowers blaze
To the horizon
There is no path
Here
You may be torn
May burn your tongue
And lips
Should you dare
To kiss

Truce

Dreamer
At the water's edge
Chalice to the ever flow
Thirst remains unquenched
In slumber
In shadow

Fish leap
Boats drift by
Content
Beneath clear skies

Valour

Flames fanned
By an unseen hand
Lick the craggy stand
No sleep
In lovely peace
For fervent man

Wealth

Blind man
What do you see?
    Yours is a rich
        And pleasant scene
   Creased is your brow
       White is your crown
Yet green is the leaf.

Rough is the tongue
  Of the dog
     Who licks your hand
Keen are its teeth
You are not the final stand
        What is to be?

Works

Through sacrifice
And silence
I became strong
Perspectives demanded
Patience
Now
In your arid
Hallowed hell
You witness the walls
Of imprisonment
Crack
Light spoils darkness

Worry

Outside
   Silence smothers
           Lame bells
The blood pulse
    In our ears
          Echoes
    The beating of wings
Fitful steps
Hollow monuments
No map
No way back
The signposts have been vandalised

LYRICS

Between tides

Immersed in the shallows of a dream
Don't know who I am but love you it seems
Little by little we walk the bridge between time and eternity

Once clinging tightly to the mast
Of a hovering ship anchored in the past
The future is hidden
Clear as light
Stark as night
It's alright
It's out of sight
It's out of sound
It's humming around

At times the sun shines not
No moon no stars
I wander through an ever lasting night
I see no life
Then see the curtains rising
To fan the ashes of desire

People see people do
People being something new
The times are ever changing
The sun still shines
Despite all reasoning
Upon the mountainside
It's so beautiful

Another siren song

There you are
Where you said you would be
Still in the shadow
Of a cemetery

Icy you
A sister to a statue
Silver and black
And smiling perfectly

Sleepwalkers pass us by
Sweet the perfume of forgotten times
But I remember goodbye…goodbye
Will I see another flaming sky

And there were dances
There was dope
There were demons at our throats
There was night
There was day
There were signposts
Leading us astray

Must we follow them
Must we heed the siren

She is calling me
To the deep and shining sea within

See within the sea within

Praying to a strange and lonely god
In the shadow of a wing
The face you made up for an age began to glow
The face you made up for an hour
Began to change

Bright Star

Softly,
Strangely,
Solemnly it seems
A thousand angels rise up high
And sing

Songs to the sky
The sea
Songs through the wind
Inside a shining eye the dream begins

She came close today
I am not afraid
So many dreams can fade in time
In time….

Bright star
Of bright day
Illuminate the way
Among the flowers ever may

Symphony of starlight
Song to distant days
Songs to the sisters of the masquerade

She came close today
I am not afraid
We can fly away forever
Forever…

Sometimes when I can hear her singing
Ringing the changes in scene
While slowly as I drown in this blue river
To watch you floating free

Green

We sat free amongst the sheltering green
Below a blazing radiant golden sun
An echo of a time that might have been
A reason for a now and time to come

A voice so gentle delicately thrown
Ascending to the clear and calm azure
Speaking sacred heart words of your own
Soulful of a spirit sure

Ten and seven silver bells are hung
Around our necks to celebrate the day
For love for light for laughter they are rung

And that there may be music on the waves
And that there may be magic on the way

And that there may be

Alive

I began where you left off
To carry the mutant around our town
To cut out their eyes
Uncover the lies
But I believe them

The circle is broken
We can't stop
I talk with the doll
My head on a pillow
I don't understand
Just stare at the ceiling
I can't just pretend
Or stare at the ceiling

I passed a child weeping into his hands
Turned my eyes
For he's so deadly
So very alive
Alive and kicking

So very alive
Alive and kicking

Amethyst belle

Amethyst belle
Wild
Pretty
Venus of the city
Inside a mellow sky I heard you sigh
'I'd love to'
But I already knew the
The tidal night would turn so soon

Promises are beautiful
Petals floating on a breeze
I hold them in my hand
They float away like dreams

Star of a stormy night
Witch angel I'm believing
The colour in your eye
Just the way I'm feeling

Who stands to judge the flowers of love?
Who stands to love alone?
Who stands to judge the flowers of blood?
Who stands to stand alone?

Promises are beautiful
Mountains move in time
Fires glow on moons and seas
Day turns into night

Talking Landscapes

Talking landscapes
Whispering trees
Dead seasons are washed away clean
The feast
The ritual
The fall and the rise
Quite a catch in nets of starlight
Catch your breath in webs of starlight
Find your head in depths of starlight

Against all odds
Through the heart of the storm
The vanishing man
At the crossroads of thought

The weary traveller in the darkness of night
Will your beloved come with the dawn
The cup
The feather
The wand
And the stone
Quite a show the shine of the dawn
Jewels you'll find in the casket of dawn
But your eyes stolen by the mirror of dawn

Against all odds
Through the heart of the storm
The vanishing man
At the crossroads of form

But your eyes stolen by the mirror of dawn

Away to your heart

You know where I want to go
I think that I know
Close your eyes
It's light inside
Don't be scared it's all right

She's strange
The moon shows her rage
It's raining again

I don't mind riding the tide
No I really don't mind

Sometimes when you're out of your mind
When you are unkind
You give a little
Take a little
Hang me high and kiss me blind

Heaven in Ecstasy

You know you have two faces
One who knows one who changes
You play games on a chequered board
Moves are made towards the dawn

You cry when you are laughing
Jokes on a scroll in the lap of time
Are silent thunder in a flickering sky
The moon and sun are one
Heaven is high

You say you hear many voices
Volume in their vanity
Multiple choices
Flowing with the river down to the sea
Crawling through the scrabble of words and deeds

The moon and sun are one
Heaven in ecstasy

Hir beautiful name

Staring into a sea of symmetry
Daydream of hir in the sun
Thinking deeper jewels dance above me
Still it won't come

Being everything and anyone to me
Got me out of my mind
Opened my eyes
Made me to see
But I lost that sight in time

Hearing voices I'd forgotten yesterday
Hear hir calling my name
Hours drifting past and floating away
Still it's the same

See I've forgotten hir beautiful name
I've forgotten hir face

Since

Today has passed so slowly
Too much time to think I think
I feed the hours mundane chores
I stare into the sink
And as I brush the dust away
From your photo by the window pane
So many people pass
But they don't mean a thing

I hear the drab drip of the rain
Its sad song sliding down the drain
I turn against this tide
It's time to dream again

The afternoon has become the morning
The evening comes to steal the light
I watch some television
I stare into the sky
I count the stars up in the heavens
Nine hundred and ninety nine
So many reasons to love you
So many reasons to cry

Summer smiles and honey kisses
In your smile I found my wishes
They had all come true
And we lived for the day

Now I don't know May from September
The frown rests heavy on my brow
Those dreams they all lie broken
The one thing I know now

You said everybody needs a lover
Everybody needs a mirror
I am so alone
Since you've gone away

We wander in wonder

We wander in wonder
The times of our lives
The thunder of the hunter
Clear in our eyes

The days' illusion so persuasive
True lies
The stories we're chasing
Just tales in time

Through that which is given
For this to survive
Uncommon decisions
A view from inside
With complex precision
And desire

You travel
Star of the day
Teardrops burn your cheeks
Water the clay
With no limitations
Your rebirth in time
Near somewhere
Near now here
In time

What

What was yesterday
What was tomorrow
What is behind the hill
What is its meaning

Electrical patternings
On a flickering screen
Formation faces
Making waves of roses

What is magical
What is the free voice
What is pointing out
What is control

What is happening
What is unfolding
What fruit is rare in summer skies where...

We were so very close
Whilst here and there we roamed
Through these misty mornings
We are ghosts
And laughing as we skipped
Through autumn dream time tripped
Into haunted houses

You Bleed (while you are dreaming)

You bleed while you are dreaming
You feed on the root of the divine
You need so much time to cry in
You lead sick dogs to blind horizons

You tear the art of love apart
You share your gold in drunk abandonment
You care for your own consideration
Beware of the bottom of the glass

Each joy with its own obvious flaw
Each toy such fun to be destroyed
Each ploy a tale of your device
Enjoy another predictable ending

So it's thanks for coming
Your time is up
You win some
Lose some
Have you given over to the rules they told you
Kisses given to the coldest shoulder

Meanwhile Gardens

Golden the light
Song on the air
I can wander and watch the sky
And the day just drifts on by

Crow cared to fly
Clown cared to cry
I can wonder and watch for signs
And the day just drifts on by

In this garden meanwhile

Skull cracks a joke
Such a funny bone

Meanwhile gardens feels like home

Out of the blue

Flying out of a winter
On bright yellow wings
Daffodil nodding
Gardenia did sing

Our laughter made ripples
In the fabric of time
Magnolia blooming
In the depth of the night

Out of the blue
You came so out of the blue

A dance deep in a wood
A dream on a lake
A fire at midnight
Hearts woven by fate

A mermaid a pirate
A high hill to climb
A soft mushroom pillow
A sweet summertime

Out of the blue
You came so out of the blue

Pale gold sun

There's a blossom
  In my heart
There's a flower
  In the dark
Spider sliding
  From my tongue
Twisted talk
  Time
Pale gold sun

Pale gold sun
  Your time will come

Thirsty forest
  River blood
Thorny clutches
  From above
Hare lit moon chill
  Sleeping one
Sweetly dreaming
Pale gold sun

Pale gold sun
  Your time will come

What circles bright
  Engage the night
What serpents bright
  Engulf the light

Sad at last

You flew through my window
A shooting star
A mystery
A flash of lightening disturbing the night

Made a glad man out of me
Made a sad man out of me
Made a mad man out of me

In my imagination
Your eyelids fluttered
Before a sea of dream
But when it came to waking up
To all those maybes ifs and buts
Those questions make uncertainty
Pulled the rug from beneath my feet
Starman magic carpet crash
Sky rocket to the ground

As the memory grows thin
I wonder when do I begin again
Who can lose and who will win?
Who can love who plays an honest game?

I can

I can

I can love you

Some future memory

I see…
I feel…
I change…

I see the sunlight reflected in your eyes
You dance the diamond night
I chase your shadow through meadows and trees
Strange life like strange life strange i

Believe in your dream
Be free in your dream
Weave in your dream

Willow we whisper wisdom of fools
Follow the path to the sea
Lullaby lover lost looking for clues
Feel to believe

Open your eyes
Open your mind
Get up off your knees

I hear you calling
New skies are falling
You know there's nowhere to hide
Your song is timeless
Your thoughts are mindless
Paradise is yours and…

Perhaps one day I'll find when I'm not looking
That there is so much to see
And the pages are turning
I'll never forget

I'm lost in a dream
Some future memory

Vampire

You couldn't open your eyes
Through the flight of summer time
Your obsession
A pure obsession
Obscure obsession
With the other side

So you can understand
The turn of the hanging man
To wear the crown
To bear the crown
To wear the crown upside down

The phoenix and the carpenter
With wings
With nails
With hammer
The jack in the joke
The jack in the joke box
The jack in the joke box
With his surprise

You walk like a vampire
You talk like a vampire
You feed like a vampire
You need like a vampire

So come on take me
So come on make me
So come on awaken me

You can count it on your calendar
Thirteen your lucky number
To walk under ladders
With your fists in your pockets
Through the cracks in the pavement
In the boring light
The pouring night
The pouring light

You talk like a vampire
You stalk like a vampire
You feed like a vampire
You need like a vampire
So come on take me
So come on make me
So come on awaken me